Booker T. Washington, seated at left, with a group of his associates at Tuskegee Institute in 1906

Cornerstones of Freedom

The Story of
BOOKER T. WASHINGTON

By Patricia and Fredrick McKissack

CHILDRENS PRESS®
CHICAGO

View of the bandstand, plaza, and some of the buildings at the International
Cotton Exposition held in Atlanta, Georgia, in 1895

Library of Congress Cataloging-in-Publication Data

McKissack, Patricia, 1944-

   The story of Booker T. Washington / by Patricia and
Fredrick McKissack.
     p.   cm. — (Cornerstones of freedom)
   Summary: Traces the life of the African American
educator and leader, focusing on his stewardship of
Tuskegee Institute.
   ISBN 0-516-04758-2
   1. Washington, Booker T., 1856-1915—Juvenile
literature. 2. Afro-Americans—Biography—Juvenile
literature. 3. Educators—United States—Biography—
Juvenile literature. [1. Washington, Booker T., 1856-
1915. 2. Educators. 3. Afro-Americans—
Biography.] I. McKissack,
Fredrick. II. Title. III. Series.
E185.97.W4M34   1991
378.1'11—dc20
[B]   91-15895
[92]   CIP
                         AC

466290

PHOTO CREDITS
The Bettmann Archive—Cover, 1, 2, 32
Historical Pictures Service—5, 12, 28, 29
North Wind Picture Archives—4, 6 (2 photos), 7,
11, 13, 15 (inset), 16, 19, 20 (2 photos), 21 (2 photos),
22 (2 photos), 24, 25 (2 photos), 27 (2 photos)
Tuskegee Institute—30
UPI/Bettmann—15
Cover—Booker T. Washington, photograph 1908

Page 2: Booker T. Washington during an address
at Tuskegee Institute about 1900

Booker T. Washington

It was September 18, 1895, in Atlanta, Georgia. Booker T. Washington, a thirty-nine-year-old Alabama educator at Tuskegee Institute, sat straight and still on the speaker's platform. A reporter described him as "a remarkable figure" with a "high forehead, straight nose, heavy jaws, and strong determined mouth."

Washington's piercing eyes moved slowly over the crowd gathered for the opening ceremonies of the Cotton Exposition. Most of the people were white Southerners, but a few Northern whites and a handful of blacks were scattered throughout the audience. Washington knew that most of them had come to hear his speech.

It had taken months of planning to get to this day. The South's economy had almost been destroyed by the Civil War and the end of slavery. The Cotton Exposition was an economic fair organized by white Southern businessmen. They hoped to attract buyers for the South's products and services.

Gallery of Fine Arts.   Government Building.   Manufactures Building.   Woman's Building.   Electricity Building.   Railroad Terminal Station.
Theatre Building.   Administration Building.   Tropical Gardens.   Horticultural Building.   Transportation Building.   Concert Hall.   Negro Building.

Wilson Avenue, Main Entrance.   Agricultural Building.   Forestry and Mining.   Machinery Hall.   Jackson Street Entrance.
Entrance to Midway Plaisance.   Midway Buildings.

C. A. Collier (below, left) was the president and director-general of the Cotton Exposition. The buildings were named according to their exhibits—Horticulture Building, Electricity Building, Transportation Building, Woman's Building.

C. A. Collier

Politically, the South was as divided as ever. In 1895, the former slaves who made up one-third of the population were at the bottom of the South's socioeconomic scale. Relations between blacks and whites were steadily getting worse, so the organizers decided to include a few blacks in the program to fend off any Northern criticism.

Washington was one of three African Americans invited to help plan the fair. He spoke before a congressional committee, requesting funds for the project. He later wrote, "I said that the Atlanta Exposition would present an opportunity for both races to show what advances they had made since freedom, and would at the same time afford encouragement to them to make still greater progress." Congress granted the funds.

For his support of the exposition, the directors asked Washington "to represent the Negro race" and speak at the ceremonies. Washington was the first black ever asked to speak at an important occasion with Southern whites. He accepted the invitation, but soon the question of what he would say weighed heavily on his mind.

The South was a racial hotbed, and tensions were mounting. Southern states were passing laws that violated the basic human rights of African Americans. Would Washington talk about that? Would he mention the increased violence against black people and the burning of their homes and their businesses? Would he demand justice and equality for all citizens as guaranteed by the United States Constitution?

Whites set fire to a school for blacks during a riot in Memphis, Tennessee.

Washington understood the social and political structure of the South. He knew that these were critical times for his people, but he took other things into consideration. "I was also painfully conscious of the fact that, while I must be true to my own race in my utterances, I had it in my power to make such an ill-timed address as would result in preventing any similar invitation being extended to a black man again for years to come."

Now the day had arrived. History was about to be made. The governor of Georgia stood. The crowd quieted. A few speeches were made. Then the governor announced, "We have with us today a representative of Negro enterprise and Negro civilization — Booker T. Washington." The African Americans in the audience cheered proudly. The whites were polite but not overly enthusiastic. They expected another "South-bashing" outburst.

Washington moved to the front of the platform. He felt sure of his message. He later wrote, "I was determined to say nothing that I did not feel from the bottom of my heart to be true and right."

First, he thanked the directors for giving blacks the chance to take part in the program. Then he told a story. "A ship lost at sea for many days suddenly sighted a friendly vessel." As the people listened

8

intently, Washington continued. The first ship's captain, thinking he was still at sea, asked for fresh water. The captain of the second ship answered, "Cast down your buckets where you are." Again there was a cry for fresh water, and the reply was the same, "Cast down your buckets where you are."

At last the captain of the lost ship cast down a bucket. When he pulled it up, the bucket was full of "fresh sparkling water from the mouth of the Amazon River." It was an allegory, a story with more than one meaning. But what did the story mean? Washington explained it: "To those of my race who depend on bettering their condition in a foreign land or who underestimate the importance of cultivating friendly relations with the Southern white man who is their next-door neighbour, I would say, 'Cast down your bucket where you are'—cast it down in making friends in every manly way of the people of all races by whom we are surrounded."

Washington went on to suggest that blacks "cast down their buckets" by providing services that whites needed. "No race can prosper till it learns that there is as much dignity in tilling a field as in writing a poem. It is at the bottom of life we must begin, and not at the top. Nor should we permit our grievances to overshadow our opportunities."

Then Washington spoke to the whites. "To those of the white race who look to the incoming of those of foreign birth . . . for the prosperity of the South . . . Cast down your buckets where you are." He called for whites to hire blacks who had "without strikes and labour wars, tilled your fields, cleared your forests, builded your railroads and cities, and brought forth treasures from the bowels of the earth, and helped make possible this magnificent representation of progress of the South."

At one point, Washington raised his hand, spread his fingers, and said, "In all things that are purely social we can be as separate as the fingers." Then making a fist, he added, "Yet one as the hand in all things essential to mutual progress."

Washington also talked about equality and justice: "The wisest among my race understand that the agitation of questions of social equality is the extremest folly, and that progress in the enjoyment of all the privileges that will come to us must be the result of severe and constant struggle rather than artificial forcing."

Washington's speech lasted less than twenty minutes. In trying to "say something that would cement the friendship of the races and bring about hearty cooperation between them," Washington told

President Theodore
Roosevelt visited the
"Negro Building" at
the Cotton Exposition.

his people to "compromise," to stop struggling for
social and political equality. Hard work, patience,
and self-pride would build their character and even-
tually earn them their civil rights.

When Washington finished, the whites burst into
thunderous applause. The governor of Georgia
rushed over to shake his hand—another first in
Southern history. According to one reporter,
"Handkerchiefs were waved, canes were flourished,
hats were tossed into the air. The fairest women of
Georgia stood up and cheered." The same reporter
noted that the black people were in tears. They
weren't tears of joy.

If Washington's speech had been delivered at another time and place, it might have been forgotten. But in 1895 the speech was printed in newspapers across the country. Suddenly, the small Alabama hamlet of Tuskegee, where Washington lived, became the center of a heated controversy.

A number of leading blacks strongly objected to Washington and his "Atlanta Compromise." John Hope, a well-known black educator in Washington, D.C., responded to Washington's compromise on civil rights: "If money, education, and honesty will not bring to me as much privilege, as much equality as they bring any [white] American citizen, they are to me a curse, not a blessing."

Hope expressed the feelings of many blacks. But what did that matter? Whites with money and power loved Washington's compromise. As far as they were concerned, Washington spoke for all African Americans.

Washington refused to debate or argue his philosophy. He let his supporters within the black community argue for him. And they did.

They pointed out that Washington's advice was sound and realistic, given the powerful segregationist movement in the South. Opposing the segregationists might create more violence—and

Carnival rides were found on the Midway. Although the Cotton Exposition was a business fair, cultural events and crowd-pleasing shows were also featured.

the blacks had no way to defend themselves. To his supporters, Washington's point of view seemed both reasonable and responsible.

No matter how history judges Washington's ideas, the evidence is clear on one point. Because of this speech, Booker T. Washington became one of the most influential black men in the world. From his desk at Tuskegee Institute, he ruled black America, dictating the destiny of millions from 1895 until his death in 1915. And even his strongest critics never doubted his sincerity.

To understand the man's ideas fully, it is important to understand the times, place, and conditions that shaped his life. "My life had its beginning in the midst of the most miserable, desolate, and discouraging surroundings," he wrote. Booker T. was born a slave. Slave birth records, if kept at all, were incomplete and inaccurate, so his exact date of birth is unknown. His tombstone at Tuskegee states 1856.

There were other important things he grew up not knowing, such as his father's name. He did not even have a last name.

The plantation where he grew up was located in Franklin County, Virginia, in a small town called Hale's Ford. The squalid conditions he lived in were commonplace for slaves. The one-room, dirt-floored cabin was about sixteen feet square.

A fireplace was used for cooking and heating. Booker, along with his older brother John and little sister Amanda, slept on rags heaped on the floor. Because there was no glass in the windows, the cabin was cold and drafty in winter, hot and stuffy in summer. Booker never had a chance to play. He wrote, "Almost every day of my life has been occupied in some kind of labour."

When Booker was too young to do field work, he

The boyhood home of Booker T. Washington stands on the James Burroughs farm located between Bedford and Rocky Mountain, Virginia. The fireplace (inset) was used for cooking and heating.

fanned the flies away from the food while the master and his family ate. Though his mother was a cook in the big house, Booker never remembered eating a family meal.

Once a week, he had a job he dreaded. He had to take corn to the mill. A large sack of corn was thrown over a horse's back for the trip. On the way to the mill, the sack often slid off. Booker was too small to toss it back up and for hours he'd sit tearfully by the side of the road, waiting for someone to pass by and help. Often night was falling before help came. But he still had to go through the dark, scary woods to reach the mill. And when he finally got home, he was punished for taking so long.

It was against the law to educate slaves, so Booker wasn't taught to read and write. But one day he saw the inside of a school. The image stayed with him for a lifetime—rows of neatly dressed children reciting their lessons before the teacher. More than anything, Booker wanted to go to school.

The Civil War ended in 1865, and so did slavery. Booker was about nine years old. His mother moved the family to Malden, West Virginia, where his step-father had found work. Booker and his brothers were put to work in the salt mines. "The first thing I ever learned in the way of book knowledge," Washington wrote later, "was while working in this salt-furnace."

Each salt packer was given a barrel marked with a number. His father's number was 18. Booker learned to recognize that number and write it. His mother encouraged him to learn more by getting

Interior view of a salt factory

him a book—from where he never knew. From that book he learned the alphabet.

At last, a school for blacks opened in Malden. But when Booker went to enroll, he realized for the first time that he had no last name. Too embarrassed to enroll, he left. But he was back the next day. When the teacher asked him his full name, he answered, "Booker Washington." He learned later that his mother had named him "Booker Taliaferro."

Washington wrote, "I think there are not many men in our country who have had the privilege of naming themselves in the way that I have." He didn't know he was following one of the oldest African customs—the right to name oneself.

While working in the salt mines and later in the coal mines, Booker also went to school. One day, he heard two men talking about a school for blacks in Virginia, called Hampton Normal and Agricultural Institute. It sounded wonderful to Booker.

Not long after, there was an opening in the household staff of General Lewis Ruffner, the owner of the salt-furnace and coal mines. The general's wife, Viola, was a Yankee woman from Vermont, known for being strict. Booker didn't care. He knew it couldn't be as hard as the mines. Besides, the pay was not bad—five dollars a month.

Mrs. Ruffner gave Booker books. Her lessons in cleanliness, hard work, and thrift, he said later, were as important to him as any education he would ever receive.

Then in the fall of 1872, Booker left for Hampton Institute. He had "no idea of the direction in which Hampton was or what it would cost to go there."

Over three hundred miles separated Malden from Hampton. Booker walked, jumped railroad cars, and hitched buggy rides. He arrived in Richmond, Virginia, hungry, tired, and dirty. He had no money, no food, and no friends. After walking around the city for hours, he crawled under a wooden sidewalk and slept. The next morning he found work on a ship. As soon as he'd saved enough money, he traveled the last eighty-two miles to Hampton.

The school was everything Booker hoped it would be—and more. As far as he was concerned, he had reached a corner of heaven. However, Miss Mary F. Mackie, the head teacher, was no welcoming angel. Miss Mackie took one look at Booker and decided he was not fit to enter Hampton. After looking at himself, Booker understood why. In his haste to get there, he had forgotten to clean up.

But Booker reasoned that since Miss Mackie hadn't sent him away, all might not be lost. After an hour or so, she sent word that the recitation room

The assembly room at Hampton Institute in Hampton, Virginia

needed sweeping. Booker understood that this was his entrance examination, and he was determined to pass it with flying colors.

"I swept the recitation room three times," Washington wrote in an autobiography years later. "Then I got a dusting-cloth and dusted it four times. All the woodwork around the walls, every bench, table, and desk, I went over four times with my dusting-cloth."

Miss Mackie inspected the room and she hired Booker to be the janitor. In this way, Booker T. Washington worked his way through Hampton—a fact that made him proud.

Miss Mackie was among a large group of Northern educators who came to the South after the Civil War to help educate the former slaves.

Samuel Chapman Armstrong, the headmaster of Hampton Institute (right), taught his students a trade or a craft. He gave them skills that they could use to get a job.

Samuel C. Armstrong

Hampton's founder, General Samuel C. Armstrong, had been a Union officer in command of black soldiers, who stayed in Virginia after the war.

Armstrong believed the fastest way to educate the black masses was through training in manual skills and crafts. Using private funds, he bought a large plantation and opened Hampton Normal and Agricultural Institute in 1868.

Hampton was a trade school. Courses included reading, writing, and arithmetic. However, studies focused on agriculture, bricklaying, carpentry, tailoring, and other such skills. Self-discipline, honesty, morality, thrift, dignity, and cleanliness were stressed constantly. Armstrong wanted to create a black working class that would provide the leadership needed to advance black people within the American society. The theory had worked for white immigrants; it could work for blacks as well.

At Hampton, female students could learn to sew, cook, or clean houses. Males learned how to set type in the printing shop (right), lay bricks, build barrels, or mend shoes.

By the time Booker T. Washington graduated in 1875, he was convinced that General Armstrong's ideas about education were the best for his people. After teaching in West Virginia and attending Wayland Seminary in Washington, D.C., Booker T. returned to Hampton in 1879. He took charge of the school's Native American students, and within the year, he was running the night school, too.

In 1881 Booker T. was chosen to start a small school in Tuskegee, Alabama. At first, the task seemed hopeless. He had very little money and no land. But Washington was determined to "build up and control the affairs of a large educational institution." He started to raise money for his school.

In 1881, Booker T. Washington used this old slave cabin (above) as an office. Washington believed in teaching students practical skills, such as farming or building, sewing or cooking.

On July 4, 1881, Tuskegee Institute opened in an abandoned church with thirty students. Three months later, Washington purchased an old plantation for $500. The main house had burned down. All that remained was a cabin, an old kitchen, a stable, and a henhouse. Within a week, Washington and the students had the old buildings ready for use.

In the early years, three women helped make the Tuskegee dream a reality. They were Fannie Smith Washington, Olivia A. Davidson Washington, and Margaret Murray Washington—Booker T. Washington's three wives.

Fannie and Booker T. had been childhood sweethearts back in Malden. After she graduated from Hampton in June 1882, they were married. She was twenty-four and he was twenty-six.

Washington doesn't say much about Fannie,

except that she was kind and gentle. She must have been patient, too. There was very little money. Many times the family survived on gifts from neighboring farmers.

By 1883 there were eight teachers on the staff. And the Washingtons had a new baby, Portia, who was born on June 6, 1883. The school limped along, surviving day by day. Then tragedy struck. On May 4, 1884, Fannie died. The medical records are unclear, but it seems she died after a fall.

Olivia A. Davidson has been called the co-founder of Tuskegee. She was twenty-seven years old when she came to Tuskegee. She had been born in Virginia and educated in Ohio, and she was an 1881 graduate of Framingham Normal School in Massachusetts.

Olivia was Washington's match as a speaker and fund-raiser, and in his words, "The success of the school, especially during the first half dozen years of its existence, was due more to Miss Davidson than anyone else." Known to her friends as "Miss D.," Olivia developed a curriculum for women that was unequaled in any school—white or black. Olivia and Booker were married in 1886. The couple had two sons, Booker, Jr., and Ernest Davidson. Though they were often separated by work and travel, the Washingtons seem to have had a loving relationship.

But Olivia had always been frail. One day, while Washington was away on a trip, a fire broke out in their home. Olivia and the children were rescued, but the shock left her ill. She died on May 9, 1899.

Washington changed after Olivia's death. His sadness was reflected in his eyes. He plunged into his work. He watched over his children.

Margaret James Murray

Then Margaret James Murray, a graduate of Fisk University in Nashville, Tennessee, joined the staff. She taught English at first, but quickly advanced to Ladies' Principal. Margaret was well-organized, smart, and pretty, but she was also bold, bossy, and outspoken. She was one of the few who dared to disagree with her boss. She got away with it, partly because she was so good at her job. And there was never any doubt that Margaret loved Tuskegee — and its president.

They were married in 1892, when Washington was thirty-six and Margaret was thirty-one.

The year after his marriage to Margaret, Washington incorporated the school as Tuskegee Normal and Industrial Institute. Using Hampton Institute as a model, he continued to teach industrial and agricultural skills, but he took the idea one step further. The staff and students helped design, build, and run Tuskegee. Student farmers grew the food

Tuskegee students built Armstrong Hall (left) and grew grapes and other foods.

they ate. Student gardeners cared for the grounds. Tuskegee became the standard by which other schools were measured.

He opened Tuskegee to all people of color. Native Americans and men and women from the West Indies, Asia, and Africa were welcomed at Tuskegee when white schools would not accept them.

Clearly, Washington's speech at the Atlanta Exposition reflected his beliefs. And if there had been no racism in the United States, it might have been possible for African Americans to advance through hard work and patience. But racism would not allow that. In 1896, the year after Washington's Atlanta speech, the United States Supreme Court ruled in the *Plessy v. Ferguson* case that "separate but equal" public facilities were constitutional. Thus, the country was legally separated by race. And, just as many blacks feared, the segregationists used Washington's words to justify their actions.

Washington remained silent on the race issue. In 1900, the year Washington started the National Negro Business League, there was a four-day race riot in New Orleans. By the end of 1901, 105 blacks had been lynched.

Controversy surrounded Washington again when he published his autobiography, *Up From Slavery*. Whites loved it, but blacks were confused. What did Washington mean when he said, "Despite superficial and temporary signs which might lead one to entertain a contrary opinion, there was never a time when I felt more hopeful for the race than I do at the present. The great human love that in the end recognizes and rewards merit is everlasting and universal." Didn't he see what was happening in his own backyard? Alabama had amended its constitution to bar most blacks from voting.

Even when Booker wrote about the Ku Klux Klan, he expressed no outrage. After describing a race riot in his hometown, he added, "I have referred to this unpleasant part of history of the South simply for the purpose of calling attention to the great change that has taken place since the days of the 'Ku Klux.' Today there are no such organizations in the South, and the fact that such ever existed is almost forgotten by both races." His critics wondered in what part of the world he had been living.

William Edward Burghardt DuBois (above) was a professor at Atlanta University. While Booker T. Washington seemed to ignore the actions of the Ku Klux Klan, DuBois could not. He was one of the founders of the National Association for the Advancement of Colored People (NAACP).

Two years after Washington made his Atlanta speech, a young black professor of history and economics began teaching at Atlanta University. His name was William Edward Burghardt Du Bois. Many of his colleagues wanted Du Bois to oppose Washington's ideas. But Du Bois held back. It was difficult to argue with Washington's philosophy of self-help and pride in one's work and race.

Du Bois grew up in Great Barrington, Massachusetts, never having known slaves or slavery. He graduated from Fisk University, and his education was radically different from Washington's. Du Bois studied Greek, French, German, ethics, political economy, English literature, chemistry, and the classics. After studying in Berlin, Germany, Du Bois came back to the United

States and became the first black to earn a Ph.D. at Harvard University.

Like Washington, Du Bois believed education was the key to overcoming racial barriers.

For years, Du Bois tried to avoid challenging Washington's leadership. Then, a series of events forced him to get involved.

Monroe Trotter, another Harvard graduate and a newspaper owner, was carted off to jail when he confronted Washington during a speech in Boston in 1903. Du Bois didn't like the idea that opposing Booker T. was a dangerous act.

Then one evening Du Bois went for a walk near the Atlanta University campus. He stopped to look at a display in a store window. To his disgust, he realized he was looking at the knuckles of a black man who had been lynched and mutilated.

These two events, plus the publication of Washington's autobiography, inspired Du Bois to write *The Souls of Black Folk* (1903), a classic in protest literature.

The book is a collection of essays dealing with African-American life and history. In Chapter 3 "Of Mr. Booker T. Washington," Du Bois challenged Washington's leadership, and asked the questions that many others had been afraid to ask.

In the tradition of Frederick Douglass, Du Bois

Frederick Douglass

stated black people's three demands: the right to vote, civil equality, and education according to ability.

The last point was a sore spot for Du Bois the scholar. Washington glorified manual labor. He sometimes made fun of blacks who studied Latin or Greek. Du Bois thought that industrial education was an excellent choice for those who chose to follow that path. But he was afraid that Washington's educational model was becoming the only option open to black students. In defense of higher education, he wrote, "Neither the Negro common-schools, nor Tuskegee itself, could remain open a day were it not for teachers trained in Negro colleges, or trained by their graduates." Then he noted in an offhand way that he'd been asked to teach at Tuskegee.

Du Bois's supporters—both black and white—formed the National Association for the Advancement of Colored People (NAACP). Du Bois was a founder and editor of *Crisis*, the NAACP magazine. At last, those African Americans who did not agree with Booker T. Washington had a leader.

George Washington Carver

Washington's supporters responded to Du Bois's criticism by pointing to the work of the great agricultural scientist George Washington Carver. In his laboratory at Tuskegee, Carver single-handedly helped revive Southern farming and created a whole new industry around the peanut.

Booker T. Washington was called The Wizard of Tuskegee by friends and enemies alike—and for good reason. His accomplishments were staggering.

Tuskegee now had more than 100 well-equipped buildings, a staff of 238, and over 1,500 students. The school had an endowment of over $2 million.

Washington spent his life working for what he believed in. His office, on the third floor of his home, The Oaks, was sunny and cheerful. Sitting behind a beautifully carved desk that was sent to him by the father of a Japanese student, he conducted the business of blacks in America. With a nod of his head, a

Booker T. Washington (left) often rode with his sons around the campus of Tuskegee Institute.

black judge was appointed. Philanthropists sought his approval before releasing funds. He was indeed the most powerful black man of his day.

Each morning Washington rode through the campus on his prize stallion, Dexter, reprimanding untidy students and faculty. He allowed students to graduate without paying all their fees—with just a verbal promise that the money would be paid when a job was found. He liked to boast that no student had ever failed to pay. It was that kind of character that made Tuskegee students the most sought-after graduates in the country.

While on a fund-raising tour in New York in 1915, Washington had a stroke. The doctors said that if he stayed in the hospital, he might have a chance to live. But Washington had been born in the South and that is where he wanted to die. The long train ride home proved to be fatal. He died a few hours after reaching The Oaks on November 14, 1915.

Booker T. Washington was one of many African-American leaders. He couldn't be the spokesman for all, because blacks, like other races, are a diverse people with differing needs and aspirations. Washington has a place in history, and history will judge his contributions. He, however, would probably like to be judged by the words of an old spiritual, "Let the life I've lived speak for me."

Although they were wrong, many white Americans believed Booker T. Washington spoke for all African Americans.

INDEX

About the Authors

Patricia and Fredrick McKissack are free-lance writers, editors, and owners of All-Writing Services, a family business located in Clayton, Missouri. They are award-winning authors whose titles have been honored with the Coretta Scott King Award, the Jane Addams Peace Award, and the Parent's Choice Award. Pat's book *Mirandy and Brother Wind*, illustrated by Jerry Pinkney, was a 1989 Caldecott Honor Book.

The McKissacks have authored over twenty books for Childrens Press, including biographies in the People of Distinction series, *The Start-Off Stories, The Civil Rights Movement in America from 1865 to Present*, and seven Rookie Readers, including three Messy Bessey adventures.

In addition to writing, the McKissacks are often speakers at educational meetings, workshops, and seminars. They have three grown sons; the oldest, Fredrick, Jr., is a sportswriter. When they aren't working on books, the McKissacks enjoy working in their garden.

jB
WASHINGT
ON

McKissack, Patricia

The story of Booker
T. Washington

466290

$13.27

DATE		